SPLAT!

starring the **Vole Brothers**

Roslyn Schwartz

Owl kids

Tum ti tum ti tum

Flap Flap Flap

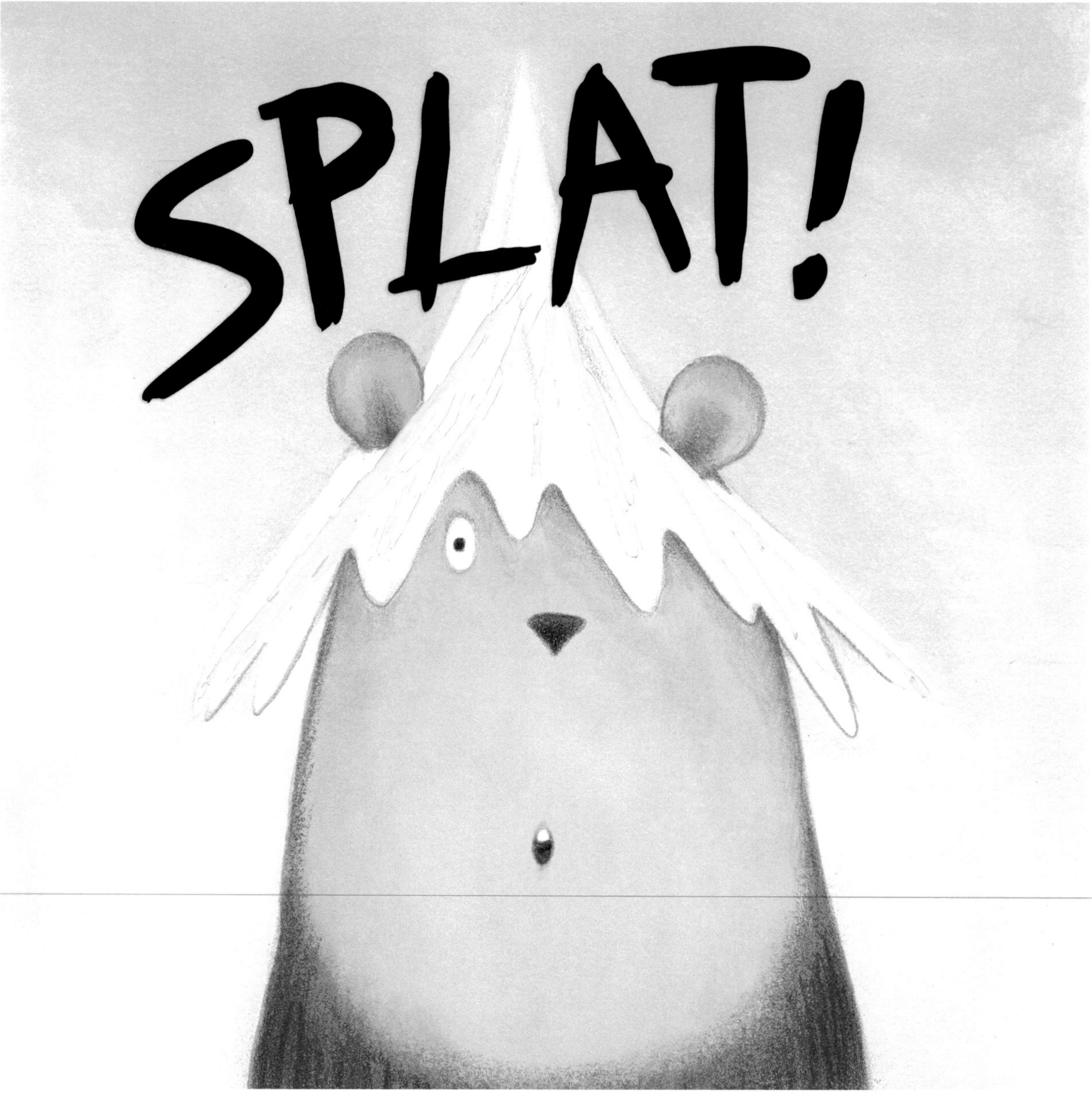
SPLAT!

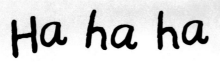

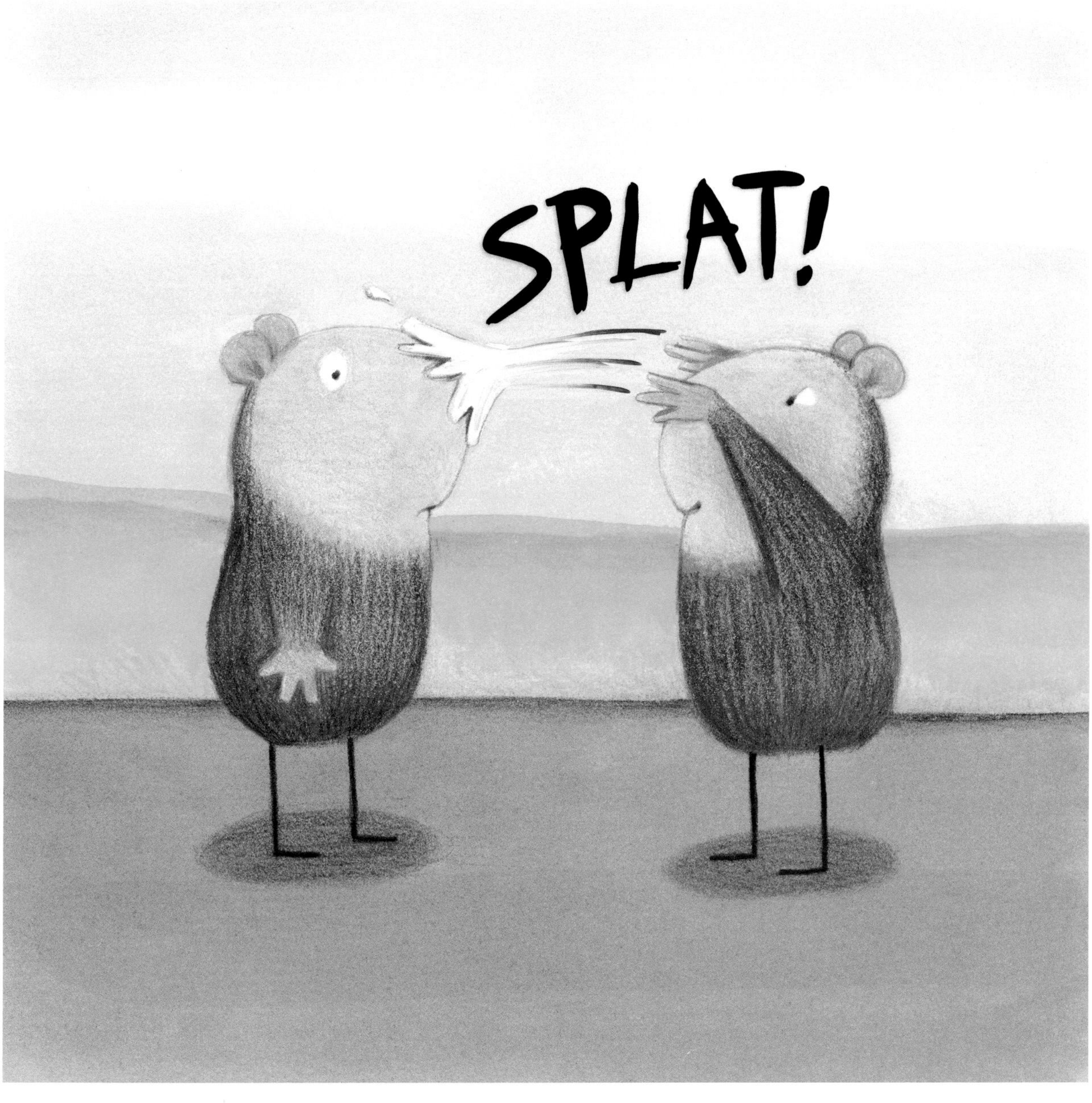
SPLAT!

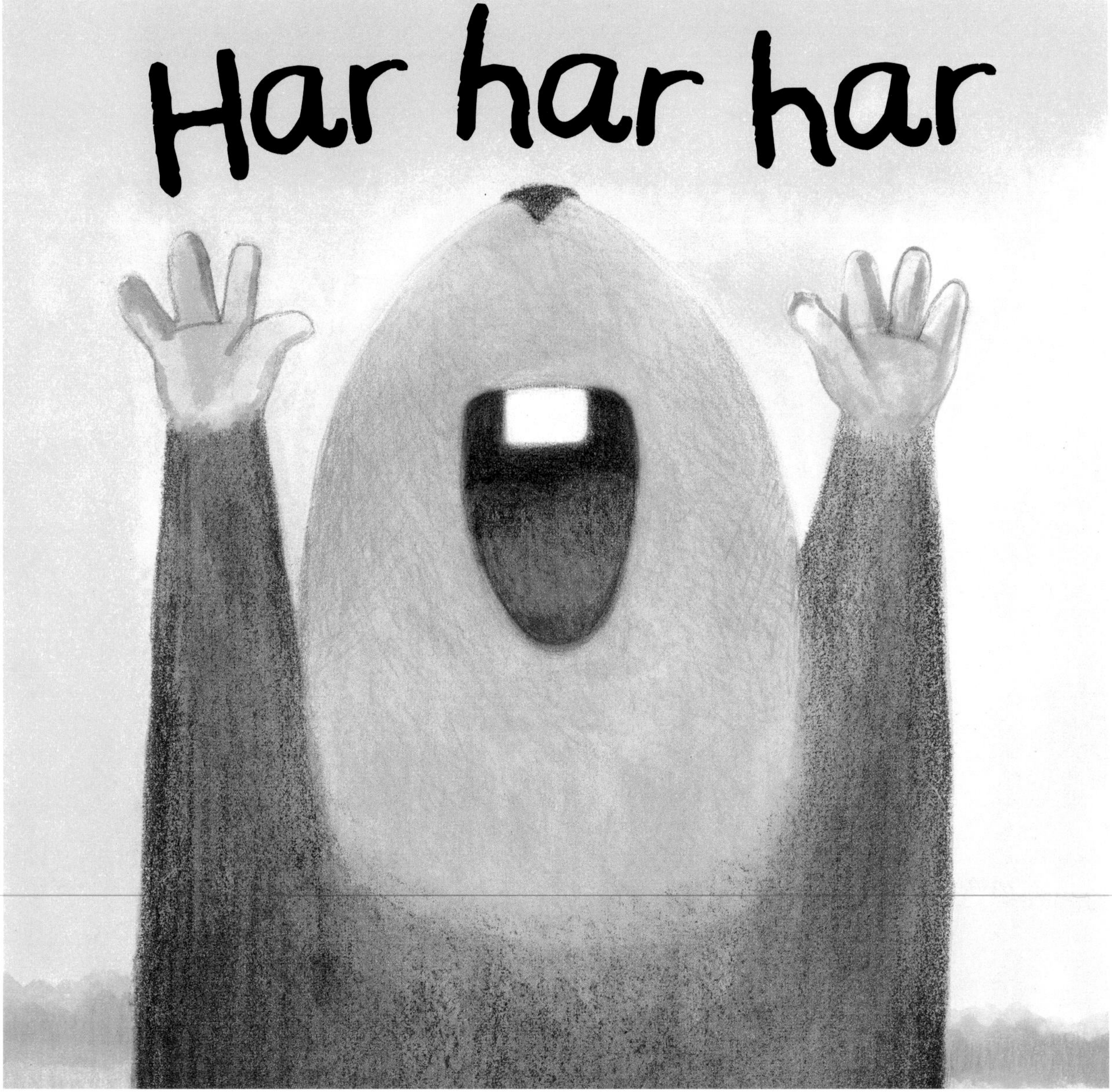
Har har har

Flap Flap Flap

Bye bye

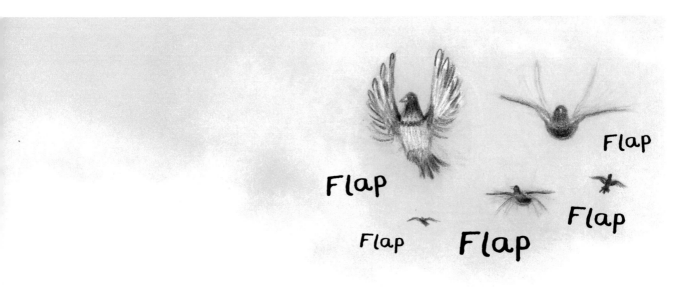

AAAARRRGGHH

Owlkids Books acknowledges the financial support of the Canada Council for the Arts, the Ontario Arts Council, the Government of Canada through the Canada Book Fund (CBF) and the Government of Ontario through the Ontario Media Development Corporation's Book Initiative for our publishing activities.

Published in Canada by
Owlkids Books Inc.
10 Lower Spadina Avenue
Toronto, ON M5V 2Z2

Published in the United States by
Owlkids Books Inc.
1700 Fourth Street
Berkeley, CA 94710

Library and Archives Canada Cataloguing in Publication

Schwartz, Roslyn, 1951-, author
     Splat! : starring the vole brothers / Roslyn Schwartz.

ISBN 978-1-77147-009-4 (bound)

     I. Title.

PS8587.C5785S65 2014   jC813'.54   C2013-904513-9

Library of Congress Control Number: 2013946675

The artwork in this book was rendered in ink and pencil crayon.
Design: Roslyn Schwartz and Barb Kelly

Manufactured in Shenzhen, Guangdong, China, in September 2013, by WKT Co. Ltd.
Job #13CB1043

A   B   C   D   E   F

Publisher of Chirp, chickaDEE and OWL
www.owlkidsbooks.com